J.E. PITTMAN

FOLIO ONE

Folio de

Trahor Fatis

Salutations, Dear Boy

T his is the story of Prince Rakozy the Uncrowned — exile, apostate, explorer of the world. Of the man masquerading as Montferrat, believed to be Bellamarre, and cavorting as Chevalier Schoening in an adventuresome youth. Of Count Weldon, he claimed, when briefly detained in England. Of he whom Francois-Marie Arouet once called *the Wonderman*. And he who continually bested that profligate philanderer Casanova at his own game. These pages contain the eagerly anticipated account of the Comte de Saint

Germain, set by my own hand, and how the mechanical godhead foretold your existence, dear boy. Of the coming of *l'Envoyé d'Éternité*.

Known as Rakozy to most in that era, this wandering wastrel was guesting with his cousin Rudolf when a particular tome corrected the course of my life. You must remember at this turning point I was as of yet uninitiated into the Mysteries and coin of my own was in dubious supply. So, when a pale sapphire the size of a robin's egg fell into my lap, I was quite thrilled with the prospect of multiplying my drinking funds with a few hands of *primero*.

Now, the saving grace was that this particular *oeuf bleu* was set into the cover of a most peculiar book of dubious provenance — upon which I shall later elaborate — but the pertinent thrust here is that, given the occult nature of the tome, my fanatically obsessed cousin absolutely would *not* let me remove the set stone…

ONE

A Balance of Needs

"I forbid it," Rudolf the Second, illustrious Archduke of Austria, King of both Hungary *and* Croatia, not to mention Bohemia — fitting, that — and of course the latest Hapsburg to titularly hold the Holy Roman Empire, forbade me. "If you desire funds, cousin," he sighed, flopping on my study settee, "the need shall be met." A magnanimous wave of the imperial hand settled the matter in his mind while his eyes lingered on the volume.

"You just want the book," I countered, knowing my cousin Rudy well. He'd always been the studious sort during our youth in Spain.

"The *Opus Majus* is slightly more than a *book*," Rudy scowled at my disregard, curling his mustache. The adornment was new to his face and my cousin still fidgeted with it. Cursed style at the time. Thankfully, my own face remained, as ever, clean shaven.

"The Greater Work of Roger Bacon as behest by Pope Clement the Fourth," I translated from Latin. "So dry," I smacked my bare lips. "*The Famous Historie of Fryer Bacon* was much more to my taste. Entertaining, to be sure."

"And less thick," the emperor mocked my light reading, coming over to peruse the gargantuan volume. Nearly nine hundred pages to crack any shelf — of which I was appointed many in my apartments. Rather much for my tastes then, really, but I was of different mind. To be expected in a Hapsburg castle, doubly so for even the most distant relation as I was, the wealth smacked you soundly in its opulent display.

Plush fabrics, the height of softness. No wall was bare, each graced with inspired frescoes of scenic vistas within the empire — some depicting the bloody battles that won it, though I managed to eschew those in my own choice of quarters — or woven tapestries heralding family history. And exquisite carvings delineated edificial, nay, monolithic furnishings likely requiring the contrivance of many machines to move.

Such were the cases of books allowed me in my study, filled already with learned treatises of every sort — among them, no small selection of other alchemical texts. Agrippa's *Three Books* fresh from the binder, selections from the Thrice-Great, the *Key*, naturally, letters from a problematic Abramelin, *The Mirror of Alchemy* — widely attributed to Friar Bacon, but believe me, it was not — and so, so many more that would come later to reform my life.

A brief aside, if you'll allow, dear boy, at least familiarize yourself with the *Opus Minus*, if none of the others. Conveys beautifully the major themes in digestible abstract.

All the alchemic texts above were copies, I do believe. Rudy liked to keep the originals for himself, and no doubt was planning to take a page from Alexandria with the *Opus* he openly coveted — copy for me, the original for he.

"Optics, mathematics, astronomy, alchemy," Rudy summarized. "Treatises on morality, philosophies on the sciences, and look," he laughed, pointing out a section, "he even proposes reforming the calendar three centuries prior."

"That thing Gregory has been on about?" Oh how little did we know. That particular Pope was a conniving bastard, wresting power back to the papacy from the corrupt cardinals — which I had to respect — and the sheer balls on him to orchestrate one of the greatest coverups, though I have my suspicions…

"The very same. Brilliant!" Rudolf was enamored. No doubt the mention of alchemy tickled his fancy, but, to his credit, my cousin was supremely generous to all the learned arts and sciences. A man well ahead of his time, in retrospect — long before I became a man *out* of time. "Whereby did you come across this treasure?"

"A gift, suspiciously enough." The parcel had arrived via courier earlier in the week. I'd thought nothing more of it until I had occasion to knock over the lumbering pile upon which I'd placed it whilst entertaining a delightful young lady whose acquaintance I'd recently made — ah, Theophania. "There'd been a letter with it, I thought," I said, rummaging through the splayed contents of the formerly lumbering pile.

"What casts such a fine gift in doubt?" At first, I'd thought the package from him — an intrigue to break my dour mood of the time — but his desirous gazes at the tome said otherwise. Rudolf had no part in the unfolding ruse.

"For one, I am skeptical of the genuine provenance. Found it," I pulled out the companion letter sealed with green wax. "I know none who use the emblem of a rampant lion set as such." I held out the envelope for his inspection.

He studied the unbroken crest, carefully running a thumb over the impression, before returning the missive unopened. "And second?"

"You're the only rich friend I have left." Truth be known, I was on the outs with everyone — family, friends, general society — after being cast from Maximillian's court in Spain. "If it came not from you, then who's left to send such extravagances?"

Rudolf thought a moment before proclaiming my reasoning on the matter sound. "Put those troubles aside for a moment," he said, reluctantly laying the book on the table. "We have a new candidate for our court," he switched to the royal we, "who claims sight of far shores and futures yet to be written."

Great, another crackpot, I wisely held my tongue. Rudy had been surrounding himself with any claiming practice of the hidden mysteries — in particular, the alchemic arts. His purpose, you might ask? As yet unknown to me.

"Let us see how your fortunes turn, dear cousin. The festivities begin once the energies of the Wolf Moon reach their peak." I was sure such a named moon had astrological significance — and it does indeed. The Wolf Moon auspices catharsis and the releasing of old patterns, as I've later become much aware — but at the time I knew nothing of that, rather that it would mean fully suffering the frigidity of that January night instead of relishing my sweet lady's warmth.

"And do grace us this evening with your entrancing melodies," he added in delighted afterthought, stroking his mustache. "For now, I feel the need to consult with Thaddaeus." Likely for another stomach ailment as had been plaguing him.

Familiar as our treatment of the other was, I was well aware of my lacking station, and so set to momentary rest the question of the book and its sender and prepared harmonious accompaniment for my imperial cousin's latest lark.

That gift, I've been blessed with since near birth. My musical ear made itself evident earlier than most, being able to replicate perfectly my nursemaid's charming lullabies at the age of three. As such, I'd developed the knack for playing the crowd as well as I played my violin, setting the mood and spirit of any whom I played before. That is perhaps my only true-born boon.

Naturally, the facility did aid in many endeavors through my many years such as when I lent my aid to darling Princess Sophie when her wretched Romanov husband's abuses became unbearable — I'd taught her the sword in her rather precocious tomboy phase and was fond of the girl, so when the letter from Russia arrived, off I went. Talk about cold, the incredibly aptly named Winter Palace may as well have been built from arctic blocks of ice! Why… I digress. Another tale, another time. There are so many to convey.

Prague in January was a cold I'd not experienced until well after I'd begun my travels in the wider world searching for the seven cities and did not relish the frost numbing my fingers upon the catgut. Entranced, I played the wiles away until my performance that night, putting thoughts of frigidity aside in favor of soaking in the warmth of a well laid fire.

"Rakozy, darling," accompanied a small knock, breaking my trance. "I can think of many better uses for those magic hands of yours," she tempted me from the doorway, as I cased my violin. "Might I offer some notes?"

"Theophania, my dear," I crossed to hold her close, placing my arms gently around the small of her back. For the era, her manner of dress was quite unbecoming of a lady — a sleek dress over thin shift, barely a stole around her shoulders to fend off the chill — but she was a woman ahead of time. "What a delightfully scandalous suggestion." There *were* indeed many other uses for such facility as I possessed — several of which I'd demonstrated previously.

She placed a hand on my chest and kissed me. "I told you to call me Tiffany," she purred. "It's all the rage in London, now. Theophania is so stuffy." Flipping her hair, she turned, taking the lead toward the downy bed. The difference between the two barely a single syllable to the ear — sounding exactly the same — but I would not raise such protest to spoil the mood.

Now, I'm not one to kiss and tell — you'll read nary a rumored whisper nor pointed sonnet regarding what occurs beyond the bedchamber door, unlike that obstreperous satyriasist Casanova — but oh how I adored the view as her delightfully round posterior swayed and shifted beneath the scant silks she wore, scarf draping suggestively as she turned back to me.

"Coming?" Her eyes the match of the most precious gems, clear and piercing — one like sapphire, the other emerald — beckoned me forward hypnotically.

"Ladies first."

Ever the gentleman, am I.

TWO

Prognostication

Oh, you'd have loved it, dear boy. Prague just prior to your claimed birth — advent, rather — was rich with marks thanks to my magnanimous kinsman. Everyone who was anyone came to the *festivities* as Rudy called them — forerunners of those balls you detest so much — if only to be seen being seen. Just so they could feel like they belonged in the world my cousin was trying to create. Most of them didn't, mind you, and soon grew weary of the airs required to keep pace when comprehension never quite dawned upon them, leaving Prague for snootier pastures requiring less application of one's intellect. But while they were in residence, oh how they spent largesse down to bare threads — bled dry in their vain attempts at couthness.

Nouveaux- and pseudo- riche alike flocked to the displays put on by those granted Rudolf's coveted patronage — quite the spectacle in and of itself. And then there were those hopefuls who dreamed of glory and wished just for the chance to catch the imperial eye. Often that chance came at a price, which station-climbers were happy to pay simply to ride those coattails to the top as well. To be thought visionary themselves for recognizing such immaculate talent.

This was how a scryer calling himself Talbot came to infect the court, but I get ahead of myself.

First though, before returning to the tale, you should know his bonafides were impeccable — his skill abhorrently real. That is to say — he trucked with demons and powers best left be.

Of similar, yet less diabolic talent — despite what many might say — my own skill with the violin was the opening showcase. The court became infatuated with the novelty of the new instrument I'd picked up on a whim after winning it in a card game. In return for not divulging his most obvious tell, the fancy pants I'd won the Gasparo off of agreed to teach me the instrument. Seeing as he'd just played to the delight of Catharine de' Medici at a court celebration, I thought maybe he knew the craft much better than the cards.

The 'music of angels' many called the sweet sounds carrying through the crystal cold night as I, in essence, played for my keep. Nothing in particular, mind you. Variations on themes from stuffier pieces, adapted by myself — typically on the fly — for the instrument as I danced among the gathered, bundled in their furs against the cold. To my knowledge, few aside from performers on the street used the violin as did I — injecting much needed energy into this particularly somnambulant crowd. Rudy's fault for holding the damn things in the middle of the night, but such were the dictates of the signs and portents his astrologers conveyed.

For me, the saltation kept me blessedly warm as many courtiers followed suit, breaking into dances of their own to match mine as I gracefully bowed out for the next musical act — being exhausted of spirit and song. There wasn't a particularly vast repertoire for the instrument, being only as old as I at the time.

"Well done, cousin," Rudy clapped my shoulder, coming close to the fire I warmed my fingers by. "You surely know how to rouse the crowd from their leaden feet." Indeed, I held great favor as his opening act at these midnight festivities.

"Always a pleasure to perform before such an esteemed group," I inclined my head. You're not the only one who lies so readily, dear boy. "Thaddaeus' ministrations set you to rights, dear cousin? You're looking healthful." A physician of the good sort, Thadd was, ascribed to the Paracelsus school of medicine — best of the era. None of that bloodletting or balancing humors mess, rather he believed in proper curatives in the form of mineral and chemical therapeutics. Rudy certainly needed one of the then modern medical establishment at his side, others having accused him of demonic possessions due to his, shall we say, idiosyncrasies — to put it delicately.

"If his earlier performance was any indication," a raven-haired stunner purred, coming familiarly close without seeming overly so, "His Majesty seems in robust condition."

"Lady Eleanor," I mocked scandal. "Such talk shouldn't be shared outside the confines of privacy, if even then."

"Hush, you," Theophania joined us by the fire, looping her arm through mine — the benefits of being uncrowned. No need to keep up appearances in public. "Dear Eleanor was just relaying the details of His Majesty's sparring duel earlier."

Where Rudy couldn't show undue favor while unwed, I kissed my beautiful Tiffany hello, taking her hand in mine, now thawed.

"Such masterful swordplay," Eleanor demurred behind fur-lined glove.

"I care only to imagine, and that under duress."

"Ahem," the emperor cleared his throat, mustache twitching. Good thing he was fond of us and in generally good spirit. "Lady Theophania, what have you to present this night?"

She was a marvel, the lady who'd stolen my heart. We'd met in the palace the summer previous, wandering the gardens was I and she intent on her study of flowering tulips. Clusius had created a wonderment on the castle grounds painting them with riotous color, only to be paled to my eye by Theophania's beauty.

A true flower amongst the weeds, I do recall saying to her. It was the first time she rebuked me, calling me names I tended to reserve for a certain someone. What can I say? I do like a challenge.

And I'd inadvertently insulted her field of study, botanist that she was — Tiffany was quite proud of her work with the Sultan's gift, under Clusius' tutelage during his tenure as the Medicinal Gardens' director.

"What I hope to be a miracle of science, your Majesty," she dipped a slight curtsy, "a frost tulip."

"We are indeed intrigued," Rudolf's eyebrow rose. The flower had exploded in popularity, and a winter varietal would be quite lucrative if properly monopolized. And, if memory serves, he'd have another good thirty years to do so. "Please," he waved her on.

"Your Majesty," she curtsied again, disentangling herself from me to take the little raised stage in the midst of the courtiers mingling amongst the warming fires. "If it be pleasing to the Crown and my eminently learned peers," Theophania addressed the crowd as porters carried to the stage a small table and a single potted plant placed beneath a large cloche — presumably in substitution of a greenhouse. The glass covering fogged the moment it reached the chilling air, obscuring the plant beneath.

The crowd murmured, gathering closer to the concealed flora, trying to peer through the condensed vapors occluding their view. I couldn't quite tell if Tiffany held the moment for dramatic pause or because she was slightly nervous. Neither of us particularly favored the limelight — quit laughing, dear boy, I speak true — but this was not about her, it was about her advancement of science, and so she bore the attention.

"I present to you a flower that fears not the frost," she placed her hand delicately upon the cover's handle, "but rather relishes in winter's kiss." She removed the fogged glass to reveal the slender slip of greenery rising from the terra cotta, terminating in an ungainly furl of dull lilac petals closed tight against the chill.

Truth be known, the bud looked shriveled and wrinkled and already expired — ready to drop at any second. My heart broke a little for her, seeing what I perceived to be a failed experiment, and a little more upon seeing Rudolf's mustaches droop in a frown.

But Tiffany would have nothing of the negativity, shining brightly in the light of the full moon as it rose higher into the night sky, bathing the stunted tulip with its secret light. Delicately, she touched a single finger to the soil of the pot.

And the miracle occurred — the tulip I thought dead began to blossom. Withered petals drank greedily in the moonlight, bursting with renewed vigor as they unfurled to the delight of those gathered — revealing a tulip of gossamer silver twinkling in the chill night.

"How marvelous!" Rudolf leapt to the stage, heavy red and black coat flaring behind him, decorum forgotten in the excitement of the discovery, only to see it wilt before his face. Silver turned tin and a petal fell as his clouding breath struck the blossom. "Did I?" I heard him whisper lightly, momentarily shocked before recovering his resolve — never show *them* falter.

"And tragic," the emperor continued for the court. "But such is the life of us all, really. We thank you, Lady Theophania," Rudolf held out his gloved hand for Tiffany. "For sharing this poignant memento mori — that even those shining the brightest may fall."

Shaken as she was by the flower's fade, she regained her composure enough to bow and touch the proffered hand to her forehead, accepting the imperial praise. "Your Majesty's wisdom is a beacon for us all."

"We look forward to your next achievements," the emperor declared, "and we remember lessons beneath the moon."

"We remember," the crowd echoed as Tiffany slipped from the stage, quietly to my side.

"I take it that went not as planned?" I whispered, pulling her aside as Rudy led the crowd in rousing oratory. He liked building pedagogical excitement among them even at perceived failure, celebrating them. Science is all about the failures, you know. The testing must be rigorous.

"It worked wonderfully before," her eyes held tears close to freezing. "The blooms lasted well into the morning before losing luster. Even his breath shouldn't have upset…"

"Those nights were not so cold as this, I do believe," I pointed to the celebrated moon, ringed now by shimmering light. "You see the paraselene, formed during this fete? It portends a thickly falling snow and soon. I imagine a few degrees variance could play havoc with such delicate systems," I reasoned of her tulip. "And

I do believe it has dropped precipitously even since this pageantry began."

"It does feel much colder," she leaned into me. "And yes," she wiped her cheek, "I was only able to hardy them down to the point of frost. This time." I adored her resolute stance.

"And now, gentle folk," Rudy finished, "the Wolf Moon has achieved its nightly zenith, and I am told by these visiting astrologers from the courts of Elizabeth the heavens have now properly aligned for this next Art."

Spies. That was the warning my cousin had just given those attending. The gala itself was sacrosanct — whatever conversations held here kept in the strictest confidences. The penalty for breaking that confidence was simple — loss of access. There were rules to these things. And manners. You played fair or not at all. It's how we did things back when espionage was a respectable affair.

Those in attendance now knew exactly what to expect from these two individuals, and how to treat them. As I said, our little gathering was protected — whatever was said or done outside those confines was on their head.

"Thank you, Your Majesty," a short man in a tall cap said, taking the stage. His beard, long and struck through with gray, gave him a wizened appearance. In fact, I do believe young John et al modeled some of that whole *wizard* thing upon this very man — Doctor John Dee. A very learned and accomplished scholar and prognosticator responsible in no small part for the term *empire* being applied to that little island which has held disproportionate sway upon history and fiction — topics at times conflated.

On the outs with Liz at the time, though, or her court, or something to the effect that he and his scryer decided it might be good for their collective health to tour Europe for a bit. So naturally they paid their respects to my cousin's court and plied their trade.

Now, I'd very much love to know how they performed their tricks, dear boy, for that is what I believed them to be. I've borne witness to many a true marvel and some cunning ruses, but not for one second did I believe what was about to take place from them — chalking it up to clever ploy and a talent for ventriloquism combined with scientific prowess, perhaps. *That,* I believed in. And oh, how I wish I could write that definitively about those two, but what took place next was no Act as you may connive.

Upon the stage with Dr. Dee, covered in blood red silks, stood what was revealed to be a mirror of obsidian crystal. Rough around the fringe from where it was hewn, about the size of a grown man's chest, but surface polished to gleam in the moon's light — and angled just so, so that it did, in fact, reflect to us the full Wolf Moon.

"As you now know who I am by reputation, at least, I'll not bore you with further details," Dee began, "but do allow me to introduce my associate here," he motioned for a taller fellow with a squirrely eye and cap close fit around his head to mount the stage, "Mr. Talbot," he called him, though later the world would know him as Kelley. "Mr. Talbot, here," he reiterated the false name, "is a man of many talents and pursuits of the alchemical and astrological variety, but he is also gifted of tongues and sight," Dee declared to many *oohs* and *aahs*.

Again, dear boy, I do say you'd love these crowds.

"And tonight, he shall be translating the language of the Angels for all gathered as we humbly seek their knowledge," Dee continued. A hush fell as the crowd listened for signs of Angels in earnest, but I focused more on the trembling hand of my darling Theophania clutching mine.

I began to ask whatever was the matter, but she shook her head, jaw clenched and eyes transfixed upon the obsidian mirror as if waiting for some disaster to rear forth from its inky surface.

"Speaking waters," Talbot declared, raising a crystal pitcher to his lips for a drink and then above the mirror's surface. "We must cleanse the portals in them for truth to be spoken." Cold as it was, I expected the water to freeze upon contact; however, defying natural philosophy, steam arose instead as the scryer poured — steam that coalesced upon the very air touching the mirror, forming a face.

A face whose sight my darling hid herself from, ducking behind my back. Dread settled in the pit of my stomach as the face moved, looking to those gathered for its viewing with burning phosphor eyes. Distasteful, sneering, barely concealing rage — these were the impressions the entity imparted upon me. Those and a surprising lack of malevolence as one might expect from such a demonic being — though briefly, as its sharp eyes lingered upon me, I felt a flash of amusement.

In truth, Theophania was not alone in her desire to be unseen — many of the ladies present and no few men, too, hid their faces, such was the intensity of the gaze. The moon herself deigned not to gaze upon the summoned specter, veiling her light in passing cloud when it did begin to speak.

Through Talbot, the visage spoke dire portents and cryptic messages — if the translator was to be believed — suggesting the rise of a 'Philosopher-King' versed in divine knowledge of the arts and sciences whose wisdom would herald universal prosperity and unlock the secrets of the Great Work for the benefit of all. A message, I suspect, crafted to impress my dear cousin.

The coarse rumble of the language and the obvious spectacle being put on sat ill on my stomach and Tiffany's obvious discomfort was excuse enough for our early departure from the rapt crowd. Though before we could make our escape, two occurrences of note:

"…and the Angel wishes it be known that as many men and women as are now have always been and shall only be…" Which sticks out to me now in memory as likely the only truth spoken by Talbot as this is the only statement the face did not scowl at, though Talbot did, and it is one corroborated by your own existence as you've explained it to me.

Second, and slightly more disturbing, the face turned at my discrete passage, regarding me as Talbot put more falsehoods within its mouth and nodded. *Free me,* I heard it speak within my own head. *Free me, ye of the Arcanum,* it said, punctuated by a small squeak from the likewise retreating Theophania.

"Did you hear it?" I tried to confirm upon our emergence from the confines.

The promised snow had begun falling, casting a hush upon the world as we walked hand in hand across a statue lined bridge. More angels, I thought, drifting with snow, seeming to float upon the night.

"I must leave you for a while, my dear Rakozy," Tiffany said of a sudden — nervous and disconcerted. Her eyes would not meet mine.

"But why?" I, myself, was shaken to brevity by such a declaration.

"Oh, my darling," she turned to face me, cupping my cheek. "There are many things to tell you and none of which I can speak," she kissed me to silence. "But suffice it to say this is not goodbye, never goodbye. Fortuna favor thee."

We parted there on the bridge watched over by angels, my heart in tatters. Blanketing snow wiping all trace of our passage.

Come morning, my darling heart had departed the castle, the city, likely the country. Taking with her only my love, the accursed mirror, and the furor of an emperor — his promise of immortality denied — and leaving me set upon a new path.

THREE

Calls the Forgotten Crown

Theophania's rapid departure from palace affairs did not leave me in the best standing with my cousin, suspect as she was in the prophetic mirror's disappearance. I begged fright at the apparition and religious objection on her behalf, though she'd never shown devotion as such before, and that she'd not dare approach the 'demonic portal' as I claimed she'd called it. That, combined with the poor showing of her botanical efforts, was enough to allay open suspicion, for a time, at least — though Dee and his compatriot took offense at the demonic allegation.

"And you know for certain it was destroyed?" This from my cousin to Dr. Dee.

"Yes, Your Majesty, most unfortunately," the doctor assured the emperor. "As you can see by my associate's eye," he motioned Talbot forward for examination, "the seal has undoubtedly been broken."

"What has his odd-eye to do with the mirror?" The eye in question, Talbot's left — which had previously been at odds with his right — appeared wholly normal and moved in concert with its mate.

"The loss of an eye was the price for…" Dee paused, choosing his word carefully, "sequestration of the Angel within the obsidian mirror."

"And since he has regained its use," I surmised, "the mirror was broken?"

"The seal, at the very least," Dee nodded. "We do hope the crystal itself remains intact as it was an increasingly rare specimen."

"Quite valuable," Talbot pitched in, targeting Rudolf. "Nearly irreplaceable." Specifically, his purse strings.

"Unlike your eye?" I couldn't help the pot shot.

"I do have two on me," Talbot said, his Irish showing. "And now both d'be working fine then." No mention of before.

"It's not unusual to trade an eye to lock a demon, angel, or other entity of the Aether in place," the doctor weighed in. "Sight for sight, as it were. The exchange equivalent."

"And now that sight is lost." Rudolf's mood darkened, glaring at the pair before turning his disapproval on me. As I said, I'd not been on his favorable side the last few months as the search for the vanished mirror commenced. "Can you make another?"

"Not so readily, Your Majesty, I'm afraid," Dee fidgeted. "We could conduct a similar ritual, ask again the favor of the Angels, but, as my associate mentioned, the mirror itself is nearly irreplaceable. The crystal essential to the process."

"Any ideas as to where we might hear word of it now, friend?" Talbot had the nerve to all but accuse me of the theft, or at least knowing of it.

Just as planned.

I'd made myself scarce during the height of my cousin's ire, to be certain, but not idle, no. Knowing him as I did, and seeing his single-mindedness on the subject proposed by the pair I suspected as charlatans, I dove into my own alchemical, astrological, and prognosticatory researches seeking a solution for the lack. In no small part due to my guilt over my lover's likely involvement, and also my own heartbreak at the abandonment, I drove myself to distraction with study, beginning with my recently suspicious gift — suddenly more keenly interested in the contents than the robin's egg jewel set in the cover.

Now, I was merely a novice at the time and while I was making progress with the texts available to me, I needed a teacher. Many an aphorism sums to the effect that when the student is ready, the master shall appear, but as you may have surmised, the ineffably inimitable Doctor John Dee — best candidate for the role — was not particularly enamored of me at that point.

Besides, he had his protege in his scryer, that selfsame Talbot, and was unlikely to take a second...

That is, without proper motivation — motivation I intended be provided by my dear cousin.

"Are there other means," I opened my inquiry, "by which one may *sequester* the intellect? Another vessel perhaps?" I had a notion thanks to Bacon's *Opus*, but the connection could not come from me — and so a bit of chicanery was in order.

Dee eyed me inquisitively as Talbot leered.

"I read of a most marvelous contraption created by Friar Bacon some few centuries ago," Rudolf chimed in. "A demonic head of sorts, I believe?"

"Why yes, cousin," I added in for flair, reminding those two of my pseudo-standing despite the recent disfavor. "I do recall that wonderment being described. And it, too, could answer questions. Have you heard of such an astounding contraption, Dr. Dee?"

"Rudimentary questions, I dare say," the doctor thought. "But yes, I am familiar with the feat of necromancy."

"Could not such a device house an Angel as well as a demon, if they are both Aetheric, as you earlier said?" Rudolf carried on my line of query — wanting answers he believed his right as emperor. The spates of digestional unrest and similar ailments having not abated with therapeutics as hoped, he sought answers from the divine — though privately, I believed he'd accept the diabolic as well, such was his distress and deterioration.

Dee considered the problem while Talbot made a poor attempt at concealing his misgivings at the matter — always wondering what angle he would take, I'd come to find out. Reminiscent of someone else I well know.

"It is conceivable," Dee allowed. "Though…"

"Then the matter is settled," Rudolf cut him off before equivocations could be made should they be forthcoming. "No doubt with your exceptional mental prowess and the advancements of the natural philosophies these last centuries since the good Friar's feat, your esteemed self should be able to accomplish this new application of your ritual."

"Your Majesty," Talbot put in his shilling. "Conceivable, yes, with resources properly suited for such an undertaking. The mechanistic workings of such a contraption alone…"

"Think nothing of it," Rudolf dismissed. "Resources you shall have, and a boon as yet in my cousin Rakozy here. Quite clever of wit and hand, if I may be so boastful. And quite eager to learn."

And that, dear boy, is how I found my way to old Londontown for the first time — in the company of astrologers and alchemists and suspected thieves, safeguarding the imperial interests under the pretense of tutelage. Suffice it to say, clever as the pair were, they found no substantive reason to disallow my presence — not after Rudolf's insistence.

As for *my* particular motives for travel, let me be plain as they are rather many — when have you ever known me to act with only one aim?

Firstly, I was intent upon proving them fraudulent in some capacity. Certainly, Dr. Dee had earned his bonafides through years of study and accomplishment in the shadows of Elizabeth's court, but there was the question of Talbot — a man whose ears had been cropped for forgery, I was to later learn, thus the cap — and his aims and influence upon the good doctor who'd taken him into confidence. Had they contrived to secret the mirror away to not only avoid deeper inspection and demands for a repeat prognostication should the act not be sound as they'd hoped, but further, mislay the blame and so claim recompense from the crown? Too, had they acted in concert, or Talbot alone?

Secondly, should their character, motives, and abilities prove genuine, I should very much like to learn last as well. I'd absorbed as much knowledge by rote as was possible in that month of study — it's no boast to say I'm rather quick in that regard — and could only further my skills by intent practice under the guidance of a master of such arts as Dee was. Talbot — I'll maintain that name for clarity of continuity, but he being Edward Kelley, an alchemist of some renown himself — as well proved an adept mentor, if but briefly, as I shall shortly relay.

And thirdly, I'd be unwise not to avail myself of such opportunity to expand my cultural horizons in general, and more specifically, should accounts of the Head indeed be sincere and not a flight of fancy, I'd be doubly foolish to not take advantage of its abilities.

Thus, after much travel with the pair — details of which I won't bore you with, though suffice it to say the mood was chilly, and fraught with tension and unallayed suspicion — I found myself at Dee's residence of Mortlake, a place steeped in history of its own, housing the likes of the Archbishop of Canterbury himself all the way to that darling of a genius Ada Lovelace before being removed in favor of a tapestry factory under Victoria. Progress is not always in good taste, especially in that regard.

It was here I gained my first course in the mysteries of alchemy, learning the basic tenets. Familiarizing myself with all the aspects — hot, cold, dry, and moist — of the Simples and the concepts of the Tria Prima essential to the teachings of Paracelsus. Obtaining a cursory understanding of the Language of Birds, basic cryptography — at which Dee was a virtuoso — and further, understanding not only the physical properties of the elements with their corresponding symbolic properties in the Great Work.

Despite all this education, though, I was no closer to discovering the secret of their trick in the palace gardens which had set me upon this course — Dee and Talbot keeping me at some distance still, despite pressing my access under Rudolf's mandate.

Meanwhile, I became absorbed in the words of the Corpus Hermeticum, the processes laid forth in the Emerald Tablet, and further ciphered the words of Friar Bacon through the lens of newfound knowledge.

"What of the original?" I asked one day, innocuously enough, poring over the

prodigious works of the monk. In the span of
some few years, he'd produced a reasonable
account of the sum of all knowledge to
that point — including the most recent
advances upon the methods of scientists,
optics and ocular importance, gunpowder,
calendrical reformation, alchemy... the list
nearly interminable. A vast multitude of words
on the collective thoughts of man committed
to the page in remarkably short time. One was
apt to wonder...

"Original what? Manuscript?" Talbot
was attempting a recreation of the head's
mechanistic workings, rather fruitlessly.
"Locked away in the Vatican or dust, likely so."

"No, the original Brazen Head." The texts
had been circumspect, certainly, but one of
Dee's first lessons had been to examine the
words left unwritten as rigorously as those
set to the page. "There is no record of its
destruction or dismantlement as there are
the ones possessed by Magnus and Pope
Sylvester." That there had been credible
evidence of additional constructs akin to that
we sought gave great heart to our search.
Though instructions for their make and use
were sorely lacking, accounts of their disposal
were quite thorough.

"What are you getting on about, Rakozy?" A resonance.

"Perhaps it exists still and we may either recommission its use or pattern our own construct upon the original if it proves no longer functional." Once made, a thing wants to be and frequently facilitates its being.

"That be a ludicrous thought, it is."

"I believe it isn't so far-fetched," I maintained. "Consider it," I waved at the amassed work of the friarly scholar upon my table, "this one man produced the work of a dozen in a handful of years. Might not he have sought the aid of the Head in this accomplishment? Even with this great accomplishment, he was cut short by his patron's death and arrested for his progressive scholarship. Might he have not secreted the device away against future opportunity?"

"If he'd been put to the question by the Church, like as not the diabolic contraption was confiscated and destroyed," Talbot dismissed my theory.

"Were that so, they'd have recorded it in their case against him, and I find no mention of it. Just 'suspected novelties' listed, which means they found nothing but hearsay attesting to any heresy."

Talbot considered my argument for a bit, chewing on the logic as much as the whiskers now growing into his mouth — a particularly bad habit of his, I'd noticed in our time together.

"Be ready at ten bells," Talbot made to leave, "and say nothing of this. I only show you should I need a second pair of hands and eyes."

FOUR

Ten Bells

A s I awaited the appointed time, I thought over our recent interplays and believed I'd begun to win the fellow over, but when I saw the room to which he led me — filled with maps of every sort piled upon each other and more still upon the wall and rolled upon racks — I saw his need of a second.

"First things first," he began picking scrolls from their nestled nooks. "Let's see if it resides in England or has awayed to the continent, if it registers at all."

Of the summoning method, I shall honor Talbot's wishes of secrecy still — I owe the fellow that much at least — but of the effect, I shall speak, as it was quite remarkable and you may benefit from its imaginativeness someday.

By binding blood to iron gal ink through their sympathies, Talbot conscripted an intellect to act as consult and wayfinder upon the various maps he produced, starting with a broad view of the country. I must confess, the unorthodoxy of the method startled me to begin.

"What have you done?" I cried, grabbing at his wrist as Talbot spilled the summoned spirit ink across the precious map, blackening the whole of the south coast of England — seemingly casting it in ruin.

"Begun the peep," he jerked clear. "Pay attention," the scryer directed my eyes to the cartomancy in play. "If the head still is, 'e'll find it," Talbot nodded at the blob spreading across the map.

Yet the ink did not stain nor seep into the parchment, rather it pooled along the surface — animated by an unnamed, to me, entity — gathering itself into puddles trudging across the charted land.

"Somerset," Talbot snapped, seeing the blob spread south and west. Carefully he unrolled the map, spreading it flat at the edge of the unblotted ink — coaxing it upon the new scape like a spider upon the hand. "Where," the diviner puzzled as the ink skittered across the page, settling into a swirl about one point. "Glastonbury, is it?"

"The ruined abbey?" Once the wealthiest, I'd read, it lay stripped of its riches and scavenged for stonework after the Dissolution some half-century prior when Henry kicked the Catholics out.

"More than that," Talbot seemed about to itch. "There are stories, but it makes no sense. Bacon was Franciscan and they Dominican."

"Dominicans were the keepers to the mendicant Franciscan seekers," Dee interrupted absently, coming into the rooms in search of something, offering his wisdom offhand before stopping cold. "What transpires here?" He stared at the pulsing ink spot upon the map, now come into his view. "What concern is it of yours, the habits of friars, that you'd break your word and imperil your soul?"

The look on the doctor's face went beyond disapproval and distaste to downright denunciation.

"And not only yours, but young Rakozy's by proxy! No," Dee declared. "I want nothing of this business. Be it on your head!"

Quick as he'd come, he left.

"What did he mean?" I hadn't yet been taught to differentiate between the Aetheric beings.

"Dr. Dee would rather I not truck with treasure demons, as such," Talbot said.

"Demon!?" Taken a moment, I cast a surprised eye at the animate blob. Not being of particularly strong faith even then, I wasn't so much worried about my soul as curious of the creature's nature. "It seems harmless enough."

Thus was my first introduction to the lesser spirits.

"Welcome to Glastonbury Abbey," the second I'd encountered — a locus, bound to place — said days later when we'd arrived. A guide, summoned as the town bell struck ten.

It didn't smell demonic. It didn't particularly smell like anything, really. Except a raven, the ruin her rookery. "Well met," said raven croaked. They have remarkable facility with words, do ravens. This one in particular more so, though, being possessed by a demon or

some-such. "The abbey is a thin place in time,"
it went on, "and you but the latest in a long line
to arrive at this place, travelers, as did I many
years ago."

"Our thanks, gracious guide," Talbot
employed the more silvered of his tongues.
Before he could continue, though, the bird flew
off.

"Some guide," I muttered, peering into
the darkness of the woods. "Why've we no
lantern?" I fumbled for my pocket strikes.

"No light, Rakozy," Talbot stayed my hand,
his voice quiet. "T'would only draw eyes and
deceive ours. The bird set our path and we shall
follow. Now be silent."

You can imagine how well I took the
admonition to *be silent*, dear boy, but needs
must when one is skulking about the ruins
of a holy place, as I would come to find
commonplace — the dead are not all that is
buried. This was the approach of the stability
loving Dominicans to knowledge, setting roots
deep in their keeps to safeguard things best kept
secret.

But that is the folly of those who tend
toward the sequestration of knowledge —
once a thing is known, it ineffably desires
to remain that way. Seeking tirelessly to

remain free, it calls to the curious and often unwary. The friars — much like the Egyptians, Sumerians, Cibolans, and many others — attempted to build prohibitions into their catacombs, intending to warn people away, but it only served to heighten intrigue and stoke the flames of desire for what lay concealed.

Unspotted and unmolested, we reached the ruined stones tumbling across the field. Humbling, the sight of what just two score years can reduce a once majestic structure to — especially when scavengers pick at the bones.

Not that I had room to speak, being one of those scavengers myself.

Talbot produced a small lantern once we came closer to the rubble, lighting the small device under the cover of stone. It was a thieves' lantern, unless I missed my guess, favored by burglars and housebreakers as the light was far more focused and directional. The small brass box housed a mirror and lens contraption surrounding a lit wick, achieving a singular beam of light shone exactly where one needed to see. I dare say the mechanisms behind this shaded light — and perhaps the motives — advanced into the modern electric torch.

A beady eye glinted in the thieves' light, setting wings to flap above an arched alcove.

The spot where a bust or figure would be displayed sat empty — either spirited away prior to the Dissolution or looted after.

"They say the bones of Arthur were reburied here." I couldn't help commentary once inside; my words had been pent long enough and seeing the history etched into the stone walls elicited them forth. Much had crumbled or been defaced, but weathering had not yet set in, being only newly exposed to the elements — relatively speaking, that is.

"People say many things," Talbot ran his hand along the frame, seeking.

"'Tis true," said I, "and each with a kernel of truth." I tried to imagine the abbey brought to life again. "That was after they rebuilt from a fire. Maybe they added a safehold?" Once, the stone walls housed countless books and treasures and were filled with people seeking to learn. Now, it housed two grave robbers and their corvid conspirator.

"Look for a switch or trigger of some sort." Talbot continued his search, the raven remaining silent.

"Would that I had eyes to see upon the dark," I quipped. Rather hard to find a secreted switch with no light by which to see or knowledge to illuminate the way.

But that indeed was the trick, as it turned out. Discovered at great peril as rotted beam gave way, crashing between Talbot and myself — the sound ringing oddly in my ears was the hint.

"The floor's hollow," I said, striking heel to stone. "In spots," I amended when the one I'd struck was of dull resonance, set firmly on thick substrata.

"What, are we meant to dig?" Talbot asked this of the silent raven.

"A test," the raven remarked — the hosting bird flapped, unsettled. "The worthy shall know the key." The spirit within remained dispassionate. A bit glib. But it had given me a further clue.

I sang through some measures of scale, pausing to listen — interrupted by Talbot.

"Quit that, what if someone hears?" Talbot demanded, light right in my eyes. "We're busted."

"If no one came at that crash," I shielded my blinded eyes. "They won't for this. Now let me listen."

Again I repeated the performance, facing around the ruin. The harmonies reflected oddly off broken stone, quite inconsistent and the technique near useless around the greater holes put in the walls — unable to retain sound.

"All these old churches were built with sound over sight, magnifying God's might through hymn, using the harmonics of the stone," I thought aloud, running my hand over the walls. "Would that I had an instrument aside my own voice, this would go much faster."

"Easier to hear changes in the resonance outside your own head," Talbot supplied, picking up my train of thought.

"Precisely my point."

"*Alas, my love, you do me wrong,*" Talbot launched unbidden into *Greensleeves*. "*To cast me off discour-teous…* What?"

I'd not known him for the musical sort, and so was caught a bit agawk by the splendor of his tone.

"Go on then," he swept his light round the room. "Listen."

Carefully, I stepped around the room, shutting my eyes to focus on the changing sounds of each stone I neared. Vaguely, I was building a picture in my head — still soft, though, nothing firm — of the abbey.

Greensleeves had ended and he was partway through *If I Was a Blackbird* — homage to our guide? — when I came upon the trick.

A bronze plate.

Cut and fit so perfect I could not even feel a seam and very much doubted I'd see one if illuminated, but the harmonics were off — that I could feel. A portion of the plate resonated differently than the rest. Unsure of how to manipulate it or what may happen if I did press — and in general wishing a view of my surroundings — I called for light, keeping my hand upon the seam lest it be lost.

"What be this?" Talbot shone the light on the tarnished bronze. Well above my hand was an inscription, worn with time's passage.

"Hic jacet something something rex *Arturius*," my eyebrows rose, "something -sula Avalonia. Well then," I laughed, raising my head to look where I knelt — what appeared to be the foot of the High Altar. "People do say lots of things," I echoed, looking to Talbot.

"Push it," he encouraged. "See what truth this kernel holds." I pressed.

Stones rumbled and ground, sliding down before the raven's niche, forming stairs into deeper darkness, diving beneath to the hollow I'd heard in the floor.

"Looks like you might be right, Rakozy," Talbot clapped my shoulder. "Monks were hiding something here to be sure."

No traps tripped as we descended the stairs — our guiding raven hopping to Talbot's shoulder as we passed, no longer speaking aloud. He risked a wider light, spreading the beam of his thieves' lamp to encompass the empty tomb.

"No one in residence, it would seem," I noted of the empty and crumbling catafalque atop a marble bier, bearing rotted once-red drapings emblazoned with a dragon — their thread-of-gold still gleaming in the dim light. "Perhaps he *did* return?" I joked.

"Someone returned," Talbot grumbled, seeing the empty chamber, his mood soured. "Cleaned the place out, I'd say."

Granted, there was little of note — the place *had* been rifled — but it was not entirely empty. Papers lay strewn about, come unbound from codices in their haste. Allow me to upgrade my description to ransacked, if you will. Whoever had been keeping secrets therein certainly removed them with haste — and I make this assertion given the thorough nature of the transport.

Had it been brigands, there'd still have been books. Had it been the church in its zealous purge, all that was left would have been put to the flame, not strewn about for our stepping upon. Seeing signs of neither, I was left with my previously stated conclusion.

Talbot seemed distracted, the raven whispering words for him alone as he knelt, reading some pages before tucking them in his pocket — from the *Book of Saint Dunstan,* I later learned when I did some rifling of my own, the prick. Fortunately for myself, I've the mind of a steel trap and once seen, it cannot be unseen, and thus I obtained the basis for the transmutation of aurum.

Oh ho! What a find! That alone should be worthy of tomes — and for Talbot in his days as Edward Kelley, it most certainly was. But here, it is but a footnote. Mostly because that particular saint's technique was incomplete, creating a fauxrum, if you will, whilst I refined the recipe at a later time — my own take adding slightly more than the bay leaves, dear boy.

"There's nothing here," Talbot frowned when he noticed my attentive gaze. "Let's go. Wasted enough time faffing about." Nervous, checking his surroundings, he made show of stuffing them in his pack.

"But what of the scry?" I asked. "Did not the spirit say the head lay here in this place?"

"They are often inexact," he admitted, his eyes roaming. "And this was *the most likely* place to find the contraption — though they did assure it once existed here." Talbot frowned as revealing the failings of his art. "Now they only lead me these," he shuffled his feet through the disperse papers strewn about the floor.

"Perhaps the parchments have some relevance to the head and that is what your spirits cling to?" I conjectured. "We should gather the lot."

Talbot seemed eager to be away. "No. Let us be quit of this place. The spirits are restless and may make their objection to our presence… more tangible."

"They bother me not, leave me light and I'll search a bit longer."

Talbot chewed his mustaches again, taking my hand. "No, I think it best to tarry not," he said, leading me to the stairs, a quickness to his step. Eagerness, rather than unease, I thought.

"Then I shall improvise," I broke free. I would not be daunted thus, by a fellow of capricious mettle or motive. And one who conjured, no less! Off I marched, ripping rotted draperies and seeking my strikes to set them alight before he could stop me.

"Wait," he called as I turned corner into darkness, but did not pursue.

Something had caught my eye earlier when
Talbot swept his beam about and I intended
to investigate. My improvised torch, now
lit, bathed the narrow corridors in flickering
orange glow which glinted off what appeared
to be an armored foot, but prone, stuck out at
odds with a corner — as if a man had fallen.

"A dressing dummy," I made it out, coming
closer. "How curious."

The foot was indeed armored, but the other
pieces were missing and there was no head
and a curious cloak draped awkwardly over the
body of the dummy, which had slumped beside
the rack where it should have been held —
knocked over in haste? At its side, a leather bag
stuffed with papers.

On a whim, I picked the dummy up when
a heavy weight hit my foot, rolling off with
a clang against the stone and coming to rest
against the wall, staring at me with one good
eye glinting in the torch's light.

"Time is," the gears ground.

"Time was," a spring unwound.

"Time is past," a clicking sound.

"Time will be," the Brazen Head propound.

FIVE

Venturesome Gains

The head, now in my possession, spoke no more after its collection — whatever remnant animation spent when the driving spring unwound. Now, I did not share my discovery nor the words it spoke with either Dr. Dee or Mr. Talbot — keeping it a secret close held after sneaking the bronze mechanism into my travel sack, dumping my extra trousers and a fine tin of tobacco to make room. I do hope the resident spirits or demons or whatever lurked about found them an acceptable trade.

"These seemed important," I said instead, delivering the parchment folio I'd collected — the bag I kept, being of fine and durable leather. Six centuries it's seen dawn now, robust as ever — to Dee's hands directly. Where Talbot was, I knew not. "Only thing resembling a book left intact," I added, describing the others strewn about.

"Hmm, indeed," the doctor made further utterances of the unintelligible variety as he thought over the papers.

"I could make neither heads nor tails of them," I offered. "They seem to be nothing more than tax records and other such ledgers."

"Of historic value," Dee mused aloud. "Superficially. But perhaps deeper secrets can be revealed yet. See here," he angled the page to the light, showing indentions in the parchment misaligned with the script. "A page unwritten."

"Unwritten? Who'd unwrite a text like this?" I was yet unfamiliar with the palimpsest as we call them today. Or, for that matter, the *unwritten* aspect in general.

"Oh many a scribe wishing to conserve resources, reusing parchments to avoid the laborious process of creating more."

"Misers and slugabeds," I sneered. Likely not those exact words, language drifts through time, but the sentiment behind them, the same.

"Not always." Dee shuffled the sheaf of parchments, looking for others *unwritten* as he'd called them. "I've taught you the Language of Birds and much of ciphers used in our trade, yes?"

"A new world open to my eyes, yes." I was unclear about the sudden tangent as he now moved to mix some vials.

"Both means to conceal knowledge." Dee spread one page flat and instructed me to fetch a fresh sheaf to write upon. "Here, we have example of another such. What better way to obscure what may be perceived as heretical than to *unwrite* it?"

"But isn't it then lost?" Sharp as I was, my mind was troubled by the notion of destroying any form of learning, though I paid strong attention to what Dee was mixing. A tincture of Aqua Gallae and Vitriol of Mars, if his lessons had stuck, creating a deep crimson hue to the blackness of the gall.

"Not so," he droppered the tincture upon the page before blotting it away. Nothing happened, at first, until he breathed upon it, adding inspiration to the words now appearing. "Quick boy, begin transcribing!"

Page after page, the secrets were revealed. Not just of mathematics and natural philosophy, but of heliocentrism, herbalism, alchemy. Further, and certainly heretical, a discourse on the creation of the Brazen Head, mechanical drawings of its inner workings, and, blessedly for my sake, the means and requirements for creating the vapors which fueled the miracle.

"You've done it boy!" Dee exclaimed. "Wonder of wonders and praise be to God Almighty for this revelation," Dee's faith slipped out, hands clasped toward the heavens.

I'd done it, alright.

So had Dee, in having me transcribe the words of Bacon's own hand, he'd cemented my advantage.

Over the next week, I periodically queried Dee on the elements requisite in the recipe — learning the means of their production, their properties, where they might be acquired, if the good doctor had a supply ready for when we built the head.

On that, he'd sent word to my cousin with the news — a bit prematurely for my taste — requesting coverage of the necessary expenditures for the construction and operation. I, too, had sent Rudy a report on the pair's activities, attesting to the veracity of Dee's findings as best I may, and relaying the unsettling news of Talbot's absence — I'd not lain eyes on the man since our return from Glastonbury.

Absently, I stared at Dee's magnificent Armilary Sphere, lost in the motion of the planets around the Sun, as he demonstrated the appropriate alignments that went into the auspicious creation of certain compounds. I know not where he obtained such a heretical wonder, but it was marvelous in both its construction and accuracy — defying the accepted wisdom of the era.

I should have been paying closer attention, as Saltpeter — one of the Simples on the list — turned out to be one such compound whose efficacy was so affected.

But I grew restless. Knowledge of the Brazen Head in my possession consumed me, tempted me — wisdom of the ages at my behest? Of course I was tempted! But also, I received a letter from my darling Theophania, breaking her long silence. Another temptation. And so, began concocting a plan by which I could attain everything.

Naïveté of youth, certainly, but damn if I wouldn't try it all over again.

First, to my Tiffany, I wrote, as I would need her aid for collecting one of the necessary Simples — six in total. Each of the *hot* aspects combined with yet another — each with purpose.

Saltpeter I've already mentioned — purchased unwillingly from Dee's stores, since I was yet unpracticed and unable to properly compound it. Dragon's Blood from the Fortunate Isles, as the Canaries were then known, was next on the list with my love's botanical aid. Beyond that, Vitriol of Venus, Cinnabar, a chunk of Ambergris, and some Hartshorn balanced the mixture.

Given your distaste for the open sea, I shall spare you the intricacies of my travel to the islands — nothing of great import happened nor any relevant detail that need be conveyed. After making my absentia from Mortlake, Brazen Head carefully concealed in my possessions, I made my way to port, hopping an island bound privateer vessel of Sir Francis Drake's fleet — which I only mention due to the later importance of that particular acquaintance in my hunt for the six cities, given his familiarity with circumnavigation.

Instead, I shall treat you to tropical vistas, my love sunning herself upon the beach, and my very first encounter with the *Obfirmata* as I knew them before your dear girl corrected my ignorance.

They call him Drago Milenario nowadays, and I caught him sneaking back to his hill one night after sunning himself on the beach too long, falling asleep mid-transformation.

"What are you?" I inquired of the Trenynn skulking through the sand. "Did you think I'd not notice if you moved but slowly?"

The tree did not respond.

"Tiff, my love," I called to her, luxuriating in the rays of the sun. "You're the expert on plants and trees and things of the green earth. Which can walk like a man does?"

"Why, none that I know, Zy," she said, joining me in my observation. The tree quivered under scrutiny. "But I'd be delighted in making one's acquaintance. We have rum," she tempted.

The tree in question, caught bare roots tiptoeing the beach, was a fine specimen of the Dragon Tree — that which we'd sought out — as we came to learn. Massive trunk braided together of branches, crowned with spiky fronds and oh so sweet smelling in bloom

— not that he was blooming then. His particular branch — do pardon the pun, it is unavoidable — of Trenynn lineage mate only every few decades. Drago was simply out to stretch his legs the night I'd encountered him.

"I do like rum," the tree replied in perfect Spanish, the language known to me — one of my native tongues. "And mine is gone," he lamented, shifting to human form — bronze skin, well-leathered by the sun, with dark hair of a medium length, sticking out at sharp angles. His eyes though, red as a warned dawn.

But not the next, clear and mild as the sun rose across the sandy divide where the land met the sea. We'd drunk through several bottles of the good stuff as the night wiled away in good company. Drago telling us of his solitude. His vigil, caring for the next generation yet to awaken, though several carried the spark.

It was these I sought, their sap creating the most potent resin of which Dragon's Blood was made.

"Careful, careful," Drago soothed the young ones as Theophania made the incisions as he'd instructed. "All will be well." It was like most such sap harvests where shallow, angled incisions are made in the bark leading down to a tap dripping into a bucket. These taps ran red with the undistilled Dragon's Blood.

"They will remember little, if anything," Drago assured us. "As but in a dream." I'd had my reservations tapping the young ones once I knew their budding sentience and asked Drago if he might consent himself.

"No, no, would that mine would work," he'd explained how once the spark had bloomed to full consciousness in the Trenynn, the distillate lost the desired effect — something to do with their transformational abilities placing them somewhere between worlds. That, or he didn't like needles.

Time is the most critical element in the alchemic arts, as you're no doubt aware by now — impetus for the theft of days yet to come and my requested form of pay. Time is the universal currency; that which we must all pay for our desires. Having a paucity of the external variety at the time, never yet dreaming what I could ever obtain, I spent mine as well as I could.

The Dragon's Blood needed time to reduce, time to distill, and time to naturally dry — forming their characteristically crimson crystals. It was at that stage the compound would be stable to transport, and it was that stage that consumed the most patience. Many alchemists lack such and try to hurry the process Via Sicca — preferring intense heat forcing the transmutation. Jabir liked to do things that way, heavy handed madman. But in my experience, while more expedient, it tends to produce far too brittle a result — hence the many flavors of projection powder. Inferior knockoffs, all of them.

I vastly prefer the Wet Way as espoused by Paracelsus and Friar Bacon, where the proper application of fundamental natural processes, given greater time, produces much more robust results. Granted, there are some exceptions, like my diamonds, which require the application of both schools in fine, harmonious balance.

"It's never going to dry at this rate," Tiffany frowned at the rain beyond our fortuitous overhang.

Nothing left for us to do in the Blood's preparation, we'd hiked to this secluded spot in the hills where a river bent on its way down to the sea, forming a small lake — perhaps a large-ish pond — before continuing on to deeper waters. Drago had shown it to us on his guided tours of the island during our weeks in residence and it was the perfect place for a private affair between lovers.

Usually.

This day, however, the clouds had been low and the humidity high — Theophania had wrapped her hair against such, rebellious golden mane that it was — with the strong scent of rain carried on the breeze, dampening the mood. Among other things.

And so, we'd dashed for the found shelter near the bend, ducking and dodging the drops as they fell — all in good fun. I mind no smattering of rain, dear boy. Invigorating at times.

"It will come to fruition when the appropriate time for it has passed, such is the way of things."

"I am quite aware of the turnings of time and bringing things to fullness, darling, but still find it vexing to be set still," she bit her lip, fixing me with her blue eye. That day, the sapphire shone brighter than the emerald, as if lit from within. Of mercurial temperament, her eyes, to change with the weather. And her mood.

"Indeed it is much like your plants bearing fruit," I latched on to the notion. "Much the same indeed," I laughed, taking in a lung full of the humid air ripe with petrichor. "Do you know, dear," I took her by the hand, stepping from the cover toward the pool, "that swimming in the rain is manifold more fun than swimming on a sunny day?"

"Come back," she pulled. "Don't be foolish."

"What foolishness?" I spun in the falling rain, laughing the fool. "Water above, water below!" I leapt toward the water as a charge stood all my hairs on end. Next I knew I felt a jolt and jumped — I don't recall ever touching the water I bound for.

"Rakozy!" Tiffany shrieked — this I judged by her expression alone as I was quite deaf from the immediate thunderclap accompanying the electrifying bolt — and ran to my side.

"Heavens," reverberated in my head, "that made my balls tingle!" Elated by my brush with cosmic forces, I grabbed up my Theophania and twirled her in the breaking storm. She cracked a mad laugh and cupped my face.

"You daft fool," her lips formed the words, muffled as my drums cleared. "How about we get out of the storm and *I* make them tingle," she kissed me. "Ye favored by Fortuna." She stared deeply at me and in her eyes, I saw a lifetime fade, wyrd light within the sapphire glowing bright.

"Delightful compromise," I kissed her back, putting the oddity from my mind in favor of the offered assignations. Multiple.

I was indeed a lucky man. More than I ever fathomed.

"What happened that night?" I'd yet to ask, preferring to let her bring it up on her own terms, but things were in motion and time began to run short, so I chose the moment carefully. Post-coital seemed reasonably favorable, if not *exactly* optimal.

"I was wondering when you'd ask," she propped up on an elbow under the overhang.

"I, too, wondered when you'd say," I replied kindly, gently running my hand over her mussed hair — come free from the frizz-staying wrappings in our vigor.

"It's complicated," she bit her lip, quite adorably.

"I expected that to be the case, but time presses and these blissful island days soon behind." Logic, ration. I often hate it. "Rudy is expecting me at court with something to show within the year. His illness grows more troubling and is demanding of answers." The mysterious bouts of affliction were both *more* frequent and *less* explicable, confounding his physicians. "Maybe sooner after I ducked out on Dee and Talbot — provided the fellow is still with the doctor," I summarized the out-falling.

"Pox on the bastard," Theophania cursed. "He tampers with powers beyond all mortal understanding. Like a child with a hot coal — not knowing the damage he does."

"Dee said as much," I recalled the map questing. "Trucking with demons and the like."

"More than that," she sat up straight. "He vexes the Arcanum with his meddling." From her tone, these *Arcanum* must hold great import.

"Forgive me, my love, but I know not of whom you speak."

"*Trahor Fatis,*" she spoke Latin, meaning roughly *Drawn by Fate.* "The triumphant ones embodying the very workings of existence. The guiding ones overseeing our growth. The *Poemandres Arcanum.*"

"Poemandres?" That name I was familiar with from my recent reading of the *Hermeticum.* Encountering it in such context gave me a new lens through which to view the text.

"That Thrice-Great fellow was apparently a familiar." Her explanation rang no bells as I could remember. "A worldly agent," she added, seeing my expression. "One contracted to an aspect of the Arcanum, granted knowledge or gift in exchange for acting on their behalf."

"Whose agent?" My curiosity was well piqued by this development. "How many are they? How does one…"

Tiffany held up a hand, forestalling my rampant inquiry.

"I don't know and care not to speculate," she fielded my querent barrage gracefully. "There are thrice-seven known of the Arcanum. As for your last, do not. It risks what Dee and his henchman have done in trapping one. Perhaps one day you'll be selected," she offered by way of amelioration, "but do not actively seek." The wyrd light was returned to her left eye.

"Unless I miss my guess," I chained conjectures together, "one has already sought me out?" Theophania stilled, breath bated. "Who or what spoke to me — rather, us? — from the conjured phantasm? You heard it as well, did you not?" None else had, but I felt her simultaneous response to the demand for freedom.

"*Il Tempo*," Tiffany released the nervous breath held deep, intentionally calming nerves — over what, I hoped to discover. "Father Time, The Wise Sage, given to wander these last centuries in reflection. That is my Lady's best guess," her clear eyes held mine.

"Old bastard always liked shiny things." Theophania's eyes glowed brightly as another voice overtook her own. Sensuous as the ocean, vast. "Always curious, asking questions of *me* — sometimes that's all I think he ever wanted from me," she sounded bitter. Former lover, perhaps? "And it finally bit him," the goddess laughed through her vessel, "right on the ass." The wyrd light faded with the laugher.

"Ahem, thank you for the illumination, my Lady," Tiffany cleared her throat. "They *were* lovers, once," she confirmed my hunch, "and, much as she'd like to leave him, she cannot allow another Arcanum to remain so indisposed. Such would throw the world's balance."

"I thank you as well, Lady…" I paused, not knowing to whom my gratitude should be directed.

"*Fortuna.*"

You must understand, this was my most direct encounter with a mystical entity, but it was not to be the last on my travels.

I parted from Tiffany upon reaching Gibraltar — she heading north on a quest of her own as I made my circuitous way east, collecting the remaining fuels. She'd been unable to free the Arcanum trapped in the obsidian mirror, only placate the entity by hiding it away — where, she told me not — until she could obtain a copy of the *Quartus* and unwork Talbot's ham-fisted conjuring. I'd seen a copy in Dee's library, I'd told her, but had done no more than skim the text, having no interest in the summoning of spirits — or of the abbreviated approach to works, which was what the *Quartus* was. A Cliff's Notes for magic — what fools!

"Fortuna smile upon you," she'd offered her Lady's blessing. With promises of meeting in Paris, I kissed her farewell.

Circuitous, I said, west before north and then east. First on the list Blue Vitriol from Minas de Riotinto. Blood-tinted waters — highly acidic — gave the mine its unique sobriquet. It was here I came across my second mystical entity in as many weeks — a displaced gnomish named Balard.

I hadn't recognized him as such upon meeting him, rather I simply saw a fellow in distress as a gang of miscreants pressed their size advantage over the poor fellow outside a cantina.

"What sport is this?" I interceded with the ruffians. "Seven to one!" I tsked at them. Tsked, I say!

"No concern of yourn," then-unnamed Balard said darkly, his lip already bleeding. "They've shorted my wage and I intend I'll have it."

"You do nothing to earn it," a bullish man spat. "You sit and you nag as we swing the picks and carry the loads."

"Dead in an hour without my *nagging* as you imbecilically put it," the gnome irate. "The lot of you! Who finds the good veins, who warns of collapse, who brings you out of the darkness sound and safe, aye?"

"We've had no need of you," a skinnier fellow spoke, lean and wiry. "There's been nary a shake or shiver in years."

"Do *you* speak to the mountain? Hmm? Hmm!?" Balard cut a striking figure. Short, but densely muscled from years of labor; his beard grizzled and bristly, shot with white about the chin that ran up to his hair, peeking out from under a blue knit cap — spilled blood staining it all. "No! Me thinks not! You ninnywhits just poke and prod and pay no mind to the signs and portents she sends you."

"*We* get the job done," the bull shoved toward Balard. Once more, I interceded — this time with poignard. Growing up in the courts, I was instructed in the sword and of most sharp things. Naturally, I prefer words to violence, but this lout seemed only to understand that particularly brutal language.

"Now," I began, "I'm certain grievances on both sides can be proven most valid, but this is not the manner in which to sort it." The bull was a head higher than me, but still I stood him down — his compatriots, too. I must admit I may have tread upon some of my noble patents in the matter to make it more trouble than it was worth to them.

"Ye shouldn't oughta done that," the mountain-talker said. "You've nae cause. But it be appreciated," he stuck out his hand.

"Call it a personal failing on my part," I laughed, taking it. "Rakozy."

"Balard," he named himself. "What brings you to these parts? Long way from home with a name like that."

"Not so far as you, I'd wager." Spaniard by way of the Scottish Highlands, unless I missed my guess. "I come for minerals critical to the transmutation of certain compounds."

"And what minerals be those?" A bloody eyebrow raised, suspicious.

"Vitriol," I said. "The blue sort come by when copper bleeds. Are you familiar?"

"Aye, boy," he grinned. "For an honest wage."

"That, I can guarantee. How about a meal as well? I'd love to learn more about speaking to mountains."

Funny little fellow, Balard, I was to learn. Did his work at night, mostly — preferring the solitude of task. I had been correct, too, regarding his homeland. A Blue Cap from Scotland, originally. A miner by calling and nature, often acting as guides to men in their caves — or playing tricks if they be discourteous and disrespectful of the mountain. Seems a trait among their kind, being cousin to those poxy Bloodybells always seeming to bother you.

Educated, too. He'd come to Spain in the company of one Michael Scot, a court alchemist to great-uncle Ferdinand a few centuries back, and settled with him for a time in Seville. A pleasant affair, I'm given to understand, but with his passing, Balard felt the call of the mountain once more and took up in the tinted river's mine.

"Let me ask you, then," I took confidence in the gnome, showing him my list. "Being associated with a court alchemist so long, might you have further knowledge of where these may be obtained?"

Balard made some faces and grumbles, running finger down the list.

"Dragon's Blood, I have obtained already," I listed what I had. "The Saltpeter as well. But I've need of the Blue Vitriol, Cinnabar, Hartshorn, and Ambergris."

"Quite the list," the Bluecap commented, handing the list back. "Not after the Stone, then?" He packed a pipe — quite novel of the time — and lit it with a blue flame from ether.

"Not as yet." Truly knowledgeable indeed. "I require these to compound fuel for a device I've uncovered." I would not share all, but the purpose of the materials may have bearing on their origin, and Balard seemed to have centuries of familiarity with such things.

"Ye'll want the natural Vitriol of Venus," he considered. "I know a place the mountain bleeds. And too," he went on, the Vitriol sorted, "the ambergris needs ta be well aged to bring out the hot nature. Fresh, ye may have figured, tends toward the moist."

"That was certainly a point of concern. The best notion I've considered is a swing through Paris' perfumeries to obtain as aged a specimen as available."

"Nae, still too fresh," Balard grumbled around his pipe stem. "Lucky for you, there be some left of Michael's."

Fortunate indeed.

"That leaves the last two." Elation began creeping into my mindset. This fellow offhandedly proved able to provide for a third of my need.

"Could be picking up the Cinnabar direct from the mines in Almadén," the gnome turned pensive, sucking on his pipe. "But a little bird warned me of some unrest." Turned out to be political squabbles in Maximillian's court over prison labor, slave trade — all of it sat ill with me. Last I recalled, Rudy had a ready supply for his pigmenters and painters from the Hapsburg mines.

"I think I can source that, if Idria will do?" I'd rather avoid my Spanish cousins for the time being — my unwelcome still slightly fresh.

"Not as potent, but aye, it'll do. As for the Hartshorn, if you're going all the way to Idria, you can hunt it along the way. Just be sure you take it when the velvet is bloodiest — just before they begin to rut."

I didn't correct him about my destination, but thanked him for the advice before parting for the night — paying his wages overdue and those for the tasks ahead.

True to his word, the next morn the diligent Bluecap had procured a full bottle of brilliant Blue Vitriol and a glass jar containing a lump of a blackish waxy substance possessed of a potently sweet earthy scent when I examined it further.

Andalusia had rewarded me richly — truly a land full of the alchemists' desire. Small wonder the Moors desired it so, leaving great stock behind when the Castilans evicted them. This was the provenance of Balard's ambergris, held in the stores of Michael Scot after his discovery of one of Jabir's holdings in bygone Al-Andalus — that place we'd come to know well, dear boy.

"*Visita Interiora Terrae, Rectificando Invenies Occultum Lapidem,*" Balard said as I examined the blue bottle.

"Visit the interior of the Earth, and by rectifying, you will find the hidden stone?" I translated, but also questioned. "I thought this the natural variety?"

"That it is," the Bluecap assured. "The mountain seeing fit to rectify the substance — a reminder to always value such patience in the work."

Two-thirds of my treasures in hand, I made for my rendezvous.

SIX

The Dog and the Wolf

Three weeks, I waited with no sign of Tiffany.

Though out of the way, we'd chosen to meet in Paris as it was known to both of us and we, as well, familiar to it. Having contacts at the University of Montpellier from her botanical studies — and by extension the Sorbonne and University of Paris itself — she'd planned to work her way through their libraries and on to others seeking the spellbook required to undo Talbot's muckery all while I collected the Simples.

I grew antsy, waiting for word, and so I started to apply my wits and nimble fingers to the other issue coming to a Head — the Brazen one. The bronze skull dared stare at me with its lone eye, reproaching me for not acting upon my worry. Jaw set at a harsh angle, it looked clenched in anger and if it had had brows, they'd have been pinched in that same emotion. The severeness of the cheeks gave it an air of reproach.

The contraption was cleverly worked, plates of different finish contrived to slide upon one another, giving the face a breath of life when it should speak — adding depth and dimension. Peering through a jeweler's glass, I could see some few workings through the tight tolerances in the plates, but enough to extrapolate the density of the mechanism from a clockwork stance. And though I wished, I dared not disassemble the device prior its fueling, lest I break something unknowing.

It had spoken four phrases when I'd come across the head rolling about the crypt floor — the words knocked loose by percussive gravity as it spent its remaining store of vapors. Had they been meant for me? Or perhaps for Friar

Bacon — presumably last to provide query — interrupted before completion.

"What drives you?" I began speaking to the head as I examined it — rotating the piece, examining it from all angles held to the light. The heft and density of the device still surprised me — even after its original encounter with my foot and hauling it nearly all over Christendom — as I manipulated the skull about. At its base were two accesses — presumably for the fuels, I'd have to consult my mental schematics — roughly where the carotids would be. Sensible enough, but there were no further accesses — only a slim receptacle where the spine should attach for accepting a support and a striking wheel at the back.

In turn, naturally, I received no response. Ironic that I needed answers — about so many things — and the very same device purportedly capable of delivering those answers remained silent. Frozen, even, in perpetual glout. Despite the static condition of the head — no matter how I worked at any of the features — its solitary eye seemed to follow my every move in a manner akin to those unnerving paintings royals love so much.

That was another mystery of the small idol — what had happened to the other eye? There was a recess in the head for a second. It did not appear to have been broken away, all the fine workings surrounding the ocular opening appeared wholly intact, but still there was vacancy — like a setting empty its stone.

So many questions with the answers held dearly inside the Brazen Head rendered impotent in my grasp.

The end of one's wits is no place to make a decision — a lesson I hope you have learned by this point, but still I reiterate — and that is precisely where my youth bade me make one. I had four of the six simples at hand — the hardest to obtain, in fact. Seemingly the most potent — and mayhap I could scrape some Cinnabar from a spot of forgotten red paint, so I thought at the time. And so, I set about producing a bastardized version of the fuel, practicing my alchemical preparations for when I must show results for my cousin.

His Imperial Majesty Rudolf the Second grew more impatient with my turgid progress reports. More distant and formal as well, his hand stilted at times — another's entirely at others — and I felt myself slipping further from his graces with only one means to return. Locked within Friar Bacon's device.

In small amounts, I used my precious Simples — dissolving slivers of Ambergris in alcohol, titrating in the Blue Vitriol as the text instructed, grinding together the crystallized Dragon's Blood with the conscripted Cinnabar and stolen Saltpeter in a pestle. Combining them all, sans Hartshorn, within alembic set over flame.

It was here I learned an important lesson — never add dry to wet, initially, especially directly over the open flame. In my eagerness and with no small amount of nerves, I erred, my shaking hand allowing a lump to splash down, eliciting an instinctive pull back which caused more powder to fall. Let me tell you dear boy, the phlogiston within the solvents and powdered saltpeter was most eager to meet my eyebrows. Energetic vapors, indeed!

If memory serves, as it usually does, the fuel for the device required a low heat to vaporize, once properly rendered, fed through a tube into one access as a vacuum was applied internally via reverse bellows — a miraculous device in its own right at the time! A feat not to be replicated for another sixty years when Evangelista upset, on accident!, a bowl of Hydrargyrum — to draw it into the device with greater vigor. Once primed so, one spun the strike wheel to kindle spark deep inside the mechanism, igniting the vapors.

Which I did.

To little effect — at first.

The device warmed ever so slightly, and the sole remaining eye took on an air of laziness. I could feel slight vibrations through the mechanism — haltingly — and I wondered if perhaps it was lacking in proper lubrication, the mechanism having sat so long. Having seen no access port for such, I was loath to apply such liberally for fear of contaminating crucial workings — the tolerances between the plates might allow application via my smallest needles.

I had little time to consider possible remedies as I found myself involuntarily repositioned across the stone floor. The memory of how I arrived there was faint at the time, but slowly the gaps filled in over the years — solid, now, in my recollection. At the time, though, all I recalled was the burning in my chest, pounding in my head, and the blinding lights behind my eyes. Others, too, I'd come to learn, experienced similar. But allow me to congeal my suppositions and collected musings in a moment.

What matters most is that the head was speaking, I realized belatedly as the ringing subsided.

"*l'Envoyé d'Éternité*," it ground, mouth softly clacking between the whir of gears. "*L' arrivée*," the words slurred. "*Le Mat.*"

How long it'd been speaking, I had not the slightest inclination, only that it declared the Envoy's arrival at some hour on the fourth day of October — by the old reckoning. Accounts of after vary, naturally, being quite a contentious day indeed. Unbeknownst to most, the days progressed in order — the fifth following the fourth as far as they were concerned — but that was not at all the case, as the Church would soon strike them from the calendar.

What mattered next most, following that vein of thought, was that shortly after the proclamation of your arrival elsewhere, dear boy, darling Theophania burst through my door in a most disheveled state and quite discombobulated.

"They're gone." Distraught. Blood wept from her left eye, duller now. "The days. How many!?" She clutched at me awkwardly, a jagged lump of sack gripped tight to her chest — digging into mine.

"Take a breath, my darling," I steadied her. "You make little sense." None to my mind, really, but the panic setting her bleeding eyes to dance softened my countenance. "From the beginning. What's happened?"

Patiently, I waited as she gathered her frayed wits and placed one event after the other.

"I made a mistake," she said to start. "The books I sought were harder to find than I thought. Not just the *Quartus*, but any of the ones Dee might have used." She shifted her grip on the bag, paying no mind to the pointed parts as she refused to release it. "My last lead turned up empty, chasing me off with a hurked fireball. Damn dragon," she muttered.

I held the obvious question come to mind for later as she went on to describe her discreet inquiries at the Sorbonne through acquaintances once her own contacts had run dry — thinking Paris' new bastion of occult learning might have acquired the texts for study. What she'd not counted on was Talbot lurking about trying to return to Dee's good graces.

"I don't know how he found me," she cringed, pausing in memory. "I was so careful…"

"One of his demons, most likely," I ventured after a moment, filling the space made by her pain to draw her back. Internally though, I seethed and began constructing scenarios for vengeance.

"How ever the manner, he took me unawares," she continued. "As he put me to the question over the obsidian mirror, I erred, calling briefly upon my Lady for some subtle aid." She drifted again, touching a delicate finger to her blood-wept eye.

"It was careless, I should have known the scryer would *see* such a thing," she bit back a curse. "Undone by my own hubris."

"Talbot is the sort easily misread," I said. "And intentionally so. Upon the surface, he seems no more than a mere swindler and charlatan given his crassness, but the currents run deep. He has no official standing among the academics — despite having studied at numerous institutions, as he attended under myriad assumed names. His whole persona is one carefully crafted to take others unawares, my dear."

In truth, it was a lesson I'd employ myself as the years wore on — becoming necessary once my face no longer changed. Begrudgingly, I have to acknowledge the impact his teachings left on my impressionable youth — serving me as well as they have — despite my disdain for the despicable man. Just goes to show that everyone you meet holds within them a truth or a warning.

"It worked," her face soured. "Weeks he held me, cut off from my Lady — a jolt like thunder wracked my mind whenever I did try to reach out. I felt so empty, being without Fortuna's good grace after so long — the silence maddening."

I held her close, hoping it comforted her. I couldn't begin to fathom such isolation as she must have felt — not then.

"I broke," she whispered. "I gave him the mirror, hoping to buy my freedom," she halted, a catch in her throat. "Or at least be released from my torment."

"But he had other plans?" The planned vengeance doubled in my mind.

"Not only could he see my Lady's touch, he could *see* Fortuna herself through me, and so desired her for himself. Would that I'd found the wherewithal to defenestrate him ereyesterday, overmorrow…" she bit bitterly at regret. "I'm so confused, when are we now? The summoning has thrown everything."

I admired the penchant for violent action my darling espoused — quite resolute — but made little sense of her misalignment of time. Also to question, what summoning?

Yours, it turns out. Well, such was the result — entirely unintended.

"It was horrible," Tiffany wept. "I felt my mind tear at the edges as I beheld Dee's folly descend." Madness filled her blooded eyes as she tried to make sense of your birth — for want of a term more fit. Arrival? Mayhap, though, did you exist before? Advent? No, but close.

The way she haltingly described the scene is as follows:

Dr. Dee and his associate Talbot, accompanied by others of their now-defunct order had attempted a summoning — trucking in powers they understood nothing of, if I may say so myself — using the black mirror and my darling Theophania as the sources from which the beings were to be extracted. Specifically *Il Tempo* and *Fortuna* — greedy bastards trying to hedge their bets. Now, whether they specifically were trying to manifest the *Arcanum* or use them to bait something *other*, I know not, just that neither happened.

Instead, in the middle of the ritual, you appeared as if by a thunderbolt struck by God himself in the wicked room. And as quick, you vanished, but not without trace.

On the grand scale, the world halted, frozen upon your arrival, though few could feel it as did I and other adepts around the world — we compared notes later on, correlating the strange portents and omens and occurrences with the selfsame date of your arrival here. Ten days sucked away from every creature that lived, by our calculation. I know, I know, you knew nothing of its doing or their dispersal — you've said as such before and I do believe you. But the fact of its occurrence remains.

More immediately, the mirror had shattered and Tiffany's eye bled.

"My Lady bade me gather the pieces even as they leaked quintessence into the ether, her voice fading." Tiffany's did the same.

The others present had apparently been rendered senseless, aiding in her escape. Time had been rendered effluent in your wake, your steps upon the world rippling further allowing her — through Fortuna's guidance — to span the distance between London improper to my hole of hiding in some few steps. Leaving all chance of mundane pursuit behind.

But not for long.

My fears proved quite founded when that rat bastard Talbot began hounding our trail. Now, the man himself was mortal, so far as I knew, and incapable of miraculous flight as Tiffany had done in her escape. His damn demons, though, gave us no rest, and with Tiffany's condition already frail, she faded as we further fled.

Menacing. Leaping from shadow — their favored ploy. Whispers in the dark if we paid them too little mind. Inexperienced as I was then, I knew not the proper ways to repel them, and my darling barely able to offer advice — what little she did seemed ineffectual as well, the world so in flux.

This worked to our favor on two occasions. Once at a river crossing in Cologne when the Rhine seemed to flow in reverse, returning from the sea to confound our pursuit. And again, as we were nearly to Prague when the stars fell drunkenly from the sky, staggering into new alignments and constellations — the heavens irrevocably altered with the theft of *Il Tempo's* horometer.

You'd begun your works, but not yet set the balance to rights.

"At least your eyebrows are growing back nicely," Tiffany teased, stroking my cheek with a weakened hand. She'd recovered, if slightly — enough to joke. "Quite thick," she ran her thumb over them, smoothing the wayward bristles.

I waggled them at her touch. The moment of levity was nice as we'd dodged the demons and surveyed the change wrought upon the world as people came to grips with the missing time — many still in denial. Took England a couple centuries to admit it and that's where the bloody theft happened! But there was no way in hell they'd take the Pope's word for it.

Stalking terrors aside, we made our way to Prague unmolested, where awaited the greatest minds of the time to solve the confounded mess, and where we brought the Brazen Head to life.

SEVEN

Of Cinnabar and Steel

With greatest apologies to our mutual friend Elder, I was glad to find a dead moose from which to harvest the Hartshorn upon our arrival at cousin Rudolf's court. Time, wonky as it was, was of the essence.

How was there a dead moose sprawled upon the stairs of Rudy's castle, you may rightly wonder? I did as well, there not having been a moose to roam the halls during my tenure. Many things changed in the world after your arrival, among them the conclave gathered in the palace to sort out the whole kerfuffle — assembled on the down-low, as it were, so as not to raise the eyebrows of conspiracy — and naturally, Tycho brought his moose.

The moose, whose name I never got, had died most unfortunately during a drunken tumble down some of the castle stairs — friend Elder is not alone in his love of a good beer if the aroma about the muzzle was any indication. Perhaps it is a trait among all moose — I'll have to ask the dear girl if she is aware.

But I digress.

Tycho Brahe had taken up residence for the season, bringing his dearly departed moose along for the ride. Dear Giordano Bruno, gone far too soon, made an all too rare appearance, if brief. Kepler himself even showed due to the gravity of the situation. The luminaries of the age had gathered to sort the stars that had fallen from our skies and shifted their orders whilst I'd snuck my way in like a thief in the night, finding myself at the wrong end of a sword.

"Damnit Rakozy," Rudy lowered his, grabbed from the wall. Blunted. More decorative than defense, but when needs must good steel always does. "I almost slit your throat." Not likely. His shoulder twitched at the motion, nearly dropping the blade. His health had slipped further in my absence.

"I have the Head." I ignored his illness defying bluster, cutting straight to the chase. "And completion is within reach, thanks to the ill-fated moose I found while skulking about upon my return. So long as you can supply some fresh cinnabar?" My eyebrow quirked at the inquiry. So did Rudy's.

"That can be arranged," he allowed. "The moose is dead? Brahe will be beside himself. Loved that moose," he shuffled in his robes toward his bedside libations — a medicinal cordial, from the smell, with an actinic twinge. "What need have you of it?"

"Hartshorn, harvested only from the antlers," I tried to soften the impact for Brahe by proxy. "Which broke during the tumble, so there would be minimal postmortem trauma to his pet." Reasonable, I considered.

"That sounds permissible," Rudolf decreed. "We shall arrange him another in recompense."

"Excellent. All I need now is Bacon's book," I examined the shelves surrounding us for the tell tale glint, "gifted to me prior to all this galivanting, which I suppose is now in your keeping?" I'd checked my former chambers whilst skulking — good word, that — only to find the book — more specifically the jewel — absent. The original anyway.

"You have the text in duplicate," he dissembled. As I suspected, my cousin had had a copy made to be left in my collection, as was his habit, keeping the original for his. "That should suffice."

"No, dear cousin, it will not. The original is needed," I held his covetous eye. "Specifically, the gemstone adorning the cover."

Theophania had confessed to *arranging* for the gift be sent to me via sources mysterious and happenstance — with Lady Fortuna's aid, of course. Not quite able to bend things to her will as do you, consciously or not — and of the jewel's importance.

"That may prove," he hesitated. Uncharacteristic. "Problematic."

"How is the retrieval of my own property *problematic*?" I twitched my brow, unease growing as I felt the menace at my heel play one over.

"It has been entrusted to a new healer by the name of Kelley, on the promise of his healing, well…" Rudolf the second raised a tremoring hand… "*this*. Seemed of particular interest to him."

"This, *Kelley*, you named him. Have you met the fellow yet?" Outrage suppressed, it would do me no good here. My cousin had grown paranoiac in my absence, given his letters and my current reception — kept at sword's length. "What of his credences and bonafides? Who vouchsafes?"

"Not as yet," Rudolf dissembled, "but Olbracht tells me he has become the talk in Elizabeth's courts for his miraculous cures and currently has her ear." In place of Dr. Dee, he neglected to add — deigning not to lump his repute with that of the fallen doctor. Things had been fractious between the twin empires, and I could see where my cousin would think twice about crossing one currently in favor. Doubly so if he could indeed cure what ailed his Imperial hiney.

Before I could make the situation worse via the commentary tipped upon my tongue, he coughed a small fit. Dim as the light was, I could see a crimson tinge bloom upon his whiskers, quickly wiped clean.

"You see nothing," he warned, rasp taking his breath.

"I see everything," I countered, concerned, "but say nothing." You tease my loquaciousness, dear boy. But I hold my

confidences tight behind the flurry of words
— a trick I've learned over a long life, entirely
counter to my natural countenance. A helpful
guise, lest you further forget.

This seemed to suffice as my cousin relented,
turning over the dull blade as another cough
wracked his chest. "You will have to take the
matter up with…" He stopped, cut short by a
cough.

Talbot, I mentally appended. It wasn't much
of a deductive leap, really. I had not just a
hunch, but a certitude of the notion locking
into place in my mind once the connection was
made. Not only was he the only one who'd be
interested, it was also exactly how the rogue
operated. And I would certainly take the matter
up with him.

Most pointedly.

Thankfully, the bastard could not resist a
duel, and on my solemn honor, I did not
instigate.

Technically.

For one can only reasonably be responsible
for their own actions and not for how others
comport themselves, is that not so? Should
I be held accountable for the fact that the
renowned Sir Edward Kelley (formerly Talbot)
was afflicted with vice for violence and a

predilection to wrath? That the man could not hold the resultant temper at my most innocuous remarks regarding his mother?

He, for one, seemed to think so. A point he attempted to press upon me with drawn steel. Solingen steel, judging by the stiffness of the blade upon contact. A good blade to be sure, though I preferred the craft of the Toledo blade works, myself. Much springier, bending evenly along the length. The bit that caught me by surprise was the dagger he parried with.

"Who'd you grift that from?" said of the Indian wootz blade binding mine with its rippling bands set to wave in the flamberge style. A veritable treasure wasted in his inelegant hand — better served in my own sinister, I rather thought.

"A blowhard who fancied himself better than," Talbot leaned in with a twist. "Common enough occurrence." An attempted dig.

Have I mentioned before my own skill with a blade? Won through earnest application of my multiple dextrosity during my indiscretionate youth at Uncle Max's court. A brutal era I'm not entirely proud of, but we all have our follies and no small measure of foibles intermingled with potentially mortal sins. Hubris among them.

But not on this particular occasion as I pressed forward and dipped my shoulder for a pass, forcing Talbot off-balance enough to disengage the dagger from both my blade and his slackened grip.

Amateur.

I say this all through the lens of memory and all applied embellishments, having not yet been quoted in treatises on swordplay nor yet had my techniques exemplified by two rather decent fellows, but it was a spiffy move.

"Fancy enough for you?" I glibbed, catching the relieved blade. Surprising how well something as basic as a tempo change can shift the flow.

But look who I'm talking to… you'd know all about that, but the lesson applies all the same.

Another is that sometimes winning is losing and that losers win well and truly in the end. A most bitter lesson as I bested the rat bastard Talbot by the blade and won my prize only to…

"We will honor the given word but wish not to see you darken these halls forthwith," my Imperial cousin no more, more like cozzonare, Rudolf dismissed my presence, gem in hand, as he fell prey to the whispers of twisted tongues before my eyes.

Even as I made my retreat from the halls, I heard Talbot wheedle and whine about losing the gemstone, only to have Rudolf call him to task.

"What need have you of the gem or book when you've already mastered the Arts required for the powder? No," he forestalled any complaint, "we move forward as promised and you'll abide our given word. Disgraced or not, he was once our cousin and I'll not…"

I didn't shed a threatening tear, only quickened my step — my path no longer twining his — wanting to remember what honor was left in my cousin as I set a new course, his esteem withdrawn for another.

Not that my cousin's favor worked out in particular for Sir Edward Kelley, as he so renamed himself. Funny how, when your tricks run out and you can't actually make more — like the projection powder Talbot stole from the crypt. Got a little too sure of himself and his position — the idiot. What errant thoughts ran through his head leading him to believe his stolen spot more secure than mine by blood? Arrogant fool.

At least for my perceived failings, I was only rendered outcast and unwelcome — Talbot turned Kelley became a rather permanent guest of my former cousin until he tried to take quite literal flight from a parapet just beyond his window.

EIGHT

Repose of the False Heart

I made quit of Rudolf's court in good order, trying so as not to make a big ordeal of the matter. Sneaky, sneaky, one might say. Amusing how when someone's trying to sneak, it draws eyes. Better to proceed with confidence and just do it, less likely to be noticed.

But look who I'm telling… few do brash confidence better than you. In recent memory, the dear girl comes to mind, and in distant, my own dear Theophania.

Ah, what a charmer. I miss her smile oh so dearly — immortalized in memory mine though the rest of her has faded with the events I will hitherto relay.

Bear with me a moment as I collect, for these are not ones I seldom visit — a sentiment I need not describe overly much to you.

"You have the correct formulation? Proper titrations?" Ever the fretter, stroking my fuzzy brow with her thumb, even as I set alembic to flame.

"My eyebrows are entirely safe this go round," I assured her, taking my love's hand. "Is your Lady smiling upon us?" Such could make all the difference in this endeavor.

Distant, her eyes now dulled, she sought Fortuna's waning favor. I looked from her to the Brazen head set on stand upon the bench — various tubes precisely fitted to their corresponding orifices, the mechanisms calibrated to feed the right ratios of the vapors into the clockwork oracle, and the azure gem to be set in the vacant eyepiece.

The obsidian mirror itself lay shattered in a prescribed circle surrounding the works, taking on iridescent shimmer of its own.

Waiting.

Wanting.

Writhing with an unlife unsettled and fractious, leaking in from the edges to form, albeit broken, the face conjured by the speaking waters during the Wolf Moon night, now seeming so long ago.

Honor thy word, Lady Luck, the words licked at my brain, slavering derision as one phasmic eye cast disparagement about.

"Someone's cranky." Wrong time for levity, I found as the Arcanum's attention shifted to me.

Weight of ages in its gaze, I fell to one knee, life unspooling before the infinite.

How unexpected... the fractured being considered the breadth of my span. It was the first time I'd ever felt so exposed, under the gaze of the trapped *Il Tempo* — threads of my life spun out far, far before me. Little did I know exactly how far they'd extend, nor did I quite fathom the preview the cranky old bastard gave. Not then. Not for a while. *...but is he worthy?*

I still don't know the answer to that one, all these years later. Or any of the other questions posed, being only half aware of the thorough scouring my lifetime was given, only the look my love gave upon coming awares once more, my head blessedly in her lap.

"Welcome back," she wearily smiled, stroking my face. A single bloody tear stained her cheek even as she tried to bring me comfort. Ever the strong one, my darling Tiffany. Even when things were at their worst, she smiled on, her own pains ignored.

"Must they be so ungentle with a soul?" Even with the entirety of seven languages at my disposal — a few additions from eleven more — I find no words to describe exactly what I felt at the violation of my entire being.

"They forget how fragile we are," Tiffany laughed, a momentary sparkle returning. "Oh so fragile." The moment lost, she carried on. "We mustn't delay. Fortuna fades." Her once sapphire eye now more than dulled, clouding inky, nearly to black.

I had no time to absorb the import of that declaration as the mechanisms within the head sprung to life. No dire prognostications as yet, the striker unstruck, only building up a head of steam, as it were, pun fully intended. Always intend them, ye cowards.

A ripple ran through the device — tightly fit plates shifting as the mechanism regained animated spark, yawning as if awakening from slumber. Casting about with its good eye, it settled gaze upon first me, then my darling Tiffany.

Startled at her sight, it screamed a resonance — unearthly yowl escaping the brazen lips, stretching too wide as my love shuddered to her soul. Shrinking. Fading, ever so slightly out of phase, she collapsed.

"Theophania," I gasped, struggling to switch place and cradle her.

"The sapphire," she weakly whispered, not correcting me. I took her delicate hand as she tried to reach, bones feeling frail now. Small sparks sprung from her fingers, popping my hand as it held hers. "Please…" she looked to me with cloudy eyes. "I need…"

Carefully, I lifted her, not wanting to release my tenuous hold lest she slip away while I fetched the gem. The jewel glowed a delicate blue, more topaz than sapphire as I brought her close, light pulsing with her shallow breath once we crossed the circle.

"Place me there," Theophania's voice said without and within, behind and a little to the left, as they always speak. Stronger, more solid as energy flowed from the stone into her clearing eye. The voice that of her Lady, Fortuna.

"That's better," the Arcanum's voice rang clear in my love's throat. Taller, she stood, solid of presence once more. "To business…"

"My Tiffany…" I interrupted, edge to my voice.

"…in no danger," Fortuna lied — a trait you share. Reassuring as you think it, it is not, as I can attest. Unwise, then, I let her carry on as she took the gemstone in hand. Crackling energy greeted her embrace, flowing up her agent's arm as the Arcanum pulled the strings.

Before my eyes, the jewel rendered clear. Colorless. Gone were the remnants of the faint topaz hue — inclusions of the cosmic. Empty. What remnant bit of Fortuna's grace seemed transferred to her worldly agent as she took my hand.

Moments flowed past, my self barely aware of each — like river rock is conscious of the current enveloping it. A revelation not of future, but of pasts echoed in the present task at hand. Friar Bacon's hand setting words to page. The myriad pieces of the Brazen head exploded on the bench, tools to finely work the metal. Every screw and plate intimately familiar to me now in the flow as if my own hands had meticulously crafted each, their operation second nature.

Everything simply fit into place, as if I'd always known. Long years of study rendered moot as the knowledge directly deposited itself — envy of any scholar and one I'd admittedly come to take granted. Thread for another time, I digress as this one threatens to come loose.

The moments that followed my revelations are eternally etched in my immortal mind, their importance lost to my ignorant youth then, firm as I relay them to you — in brief as my borrowed time runs short.

We succeeded in the summoning — giving refuge to the Arcanum temporarily within the jewel. Not that there was a doubt once Fortuna spent her graces ensuring the pyrrhic victory came to pass. Noble as it was and I suppose important to the grand scheme of cosmic endeavors that Father Time be released from phasmic form trapped within the obsidian mirror shards. Given the chance, I'd not again.

The price, mine paid, too great even for what was received — no mere eye exchanged for sight, no. For you see, as I focused on the transference, my love, my heart, my beloved Theophania ceased. Blinded as I was by the scouring energies released, deafened by the rush of time, rendered nigh on numb and senseless by the force of an absolute *presence* in the universe, I felt her loving warmth as the merest whisper — "…my love is yours, now and once yet to come…" behind me and a little to the left, a parting plea "…find the fortunate son."

Fare Thee Well

That would be you, dear boy. *Trahor Fatis,* the Envoy of Eternity, emissary of the Arcanum drawn here by Fate herself — fool that you are.

Fortuna faded and time unthread. Freed, but not unchanged, as I was come to learn these centuries hence. Time makes hermits of us all, as *Il Tempo* became — residing now within the Brazen Head — as those we come to love fade, ephemeral as flowers. Spent petals by the side of our lives' paths.

Symptom of the Immortal — you well knew, once…

"Grief is the unspent love we carry for those lost," the Hermit counseled when I asked his thoughts in a moment of weakened resolve. But I press on for my love for her, still unspent outweighs the onward press of time.

Maybe again.

And so I draw this missive, this recounting a chapter of my life to an end. These untold tears I've held in check since threaten and the reason I've never brought her to your attention now laid plain — as, unlike some, I chose not to wear my heart upon my sleeve.

But I leave you with this, dear boy: Find my heart's wife, or I will burn it all to the ground.

Be An Indie Hero

Thanks for supporting an indie author – YOU ROCK!!

But you know, there are four easy ways to help even more – if you feel like being a bit extra (and who doesn't, really?)

1. Follow me on my socials and say hi! Also sign up for my newsletter. Like and share my stuff, you know the drill by now. Also tag me when you start reading my book! The more engagement, the wider the reach.

2. Review the book. You would not believe just how much that really helps! Social proof is totally a thing and if you

say my book is cool, others are going to listen. Can be a simple "I loved it!"

3. TELL EVERYONE! Corollary to the reviews are recommendations. Be like: "You have to read this book, I need someone to talk about it with!" See someone looking for a book like mine online? Point them my way. Or hey, start up a book club. I'm totally down to chat about my books.

4. Buy my next book! If you liked the one you got, I have several coming out each year to thrill and delight you! You can also request my books get added to your local bookstore or library. That'd be a huge help!

Again, thank you for being an indie hero! Every bit helps an author like me.

If you'd like to go ahead and sign up for my newsletter, just visit halfacrepond.com/newsletter/or scan the QR.

Also By

<u>Felixverse</u>
Felix Chance
Second Chance
Off Chance
<u>Science Fiction</u>
Pandora Squad
<u>Anthologies</u>
"Into the Fire" in *Hidden Villains Arise*
"The Iron Sigh" in *Behind the Shadows*
<u>Humor</u>
98 Rabbits: An Assemblage of Words

About

J.E. Pittman is
an author dabbling
in many speculative
worlds. He blurs the
borders between genre
and crafts salient lies
to tell a measure
of truth. His work
has been described as:
capriciously chimeric,
dreamlike, and a vivid

enigma with indelible images stamped on
your brain. Discover more of his words on
halfacrepond.com